Town Mouse and Cou

An Aesop's Fable

retold by Cynthia Swain

illustrated by Bill Greenhead

Town Mouse and Country Mouse
were cousins. Growing up, they
spent summers together.

They were close, but they had different opinions. Each mouse believed where he lived was the best place on Earth.

"The country is better than the town," said Country Mouse. "Come over and you will see."

Town Mouse went to
Country Mouse's farm.
It was harvest time.
Country Mouse had
big piles of corn,
carrots, and beans.

"Country Mouse," said Town Mouse,
"you work like a dog. Why do
you work so hard?"

"I need to have good food for winter,"
said Country Mouse. "Look how much I have
stored up. This is why the country is better
than the town. Don't you agree?"

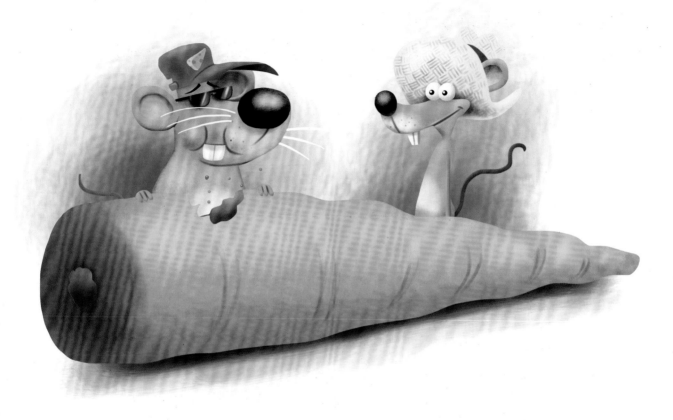

Town Mouse said, "Let me taste your food.
Then I will answer." He took a few bites and
then twitched his nose.

"Well?" said Country Mouse. "What do you think?"

"You do have lots of food in the country," Town Mouse said. "But it is so plain. The town food is tastier. Visit me and I will show you."

Country Mouse visited the town. Town
Mouse was determined to show Country
Mouse that the town was the best place.
They went to a trash can.

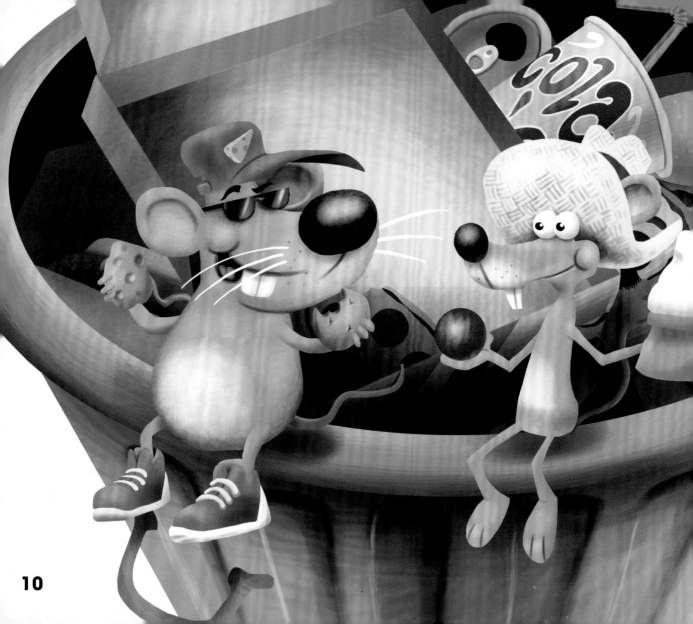

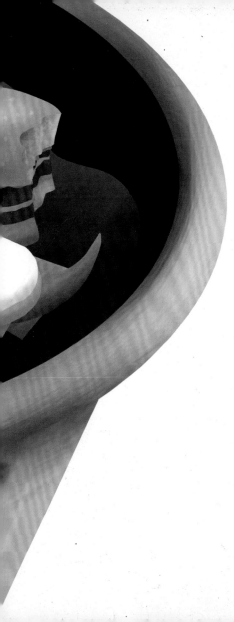

"At night, people leave this food here," said Town Mouse. "I don't have to work for my food like you do. Look—there's pizza. There's cake! Yum!"

The two cousins jumped into the can. The food was tasty. Country Mouse ate everything. "You were right!" said Country Mouse. "That was delicious. That was the tastiest food I have ever eaten."

Town Mouse said, "Say it, Cousin. The town is better than the country."

Suddenly the mice heard a noise coming toward them. Country Mouse was scared. "What is that?" he asked.

"Why, you're afraid of your own shadow!" said Town Mouse. "In the town, there are many scary noises. They sound bad. But do not worry."

The sound grew closer. It grew louder. Country Mouse's heart beat quickly.

"I may be from the country, but that's not just a noise. That's a cat!"

"Yes, it is," said Town Mouse.
"Every night the cat tries to catch me.
Every night I run away. It's fun!"

"Not to me!" cried Country Mouse.
"I do not like that game."
He ran out from the trash can.
He ran all the way home.

The town had a lot of good food that was easy to get. But in the country, he was safe from cats.

Moral: It is better to work hard and live in peace, than to barely work and live in fear.